www.enchantedlion.com

First English-language edition published in 2021 by Enchanted Lion Books
248 Creamer Street, Studio 4, Brooklyn, NY 11231
First published in Japan in 2018 as *Kuroino* by KAISEI-SHA Publishing Co., Ltd., Tokyo
Japanese edition copyright © 2018 by Kiyo Tanaka
English-language translation copyright © 2021 by David Boyd
English translation rights arranged with KAISEI-SHA Publishing Co., Ltd.
through Japan Foreign-Rights Centre
Editor, English-language text: Claudia Zoe Bedrick
Design: Lawrence Kim
All rights reserved under International and Pan-American Copyright Conventions

ISBN: 978-1-59270-358-6

Printed in China by RR Donnelley Asia Printing Solutions Ltd.
First Printing

The Little One

Kiyo Tanaka

Translated from Japanese by David Boyd

Enchanted Lion Books
NEW YORK

On my way home,
I see a little figure up on the wall.

What is it doing?

The next time I see it,
it's sitting at a bus stop.

There it is again!
I'm going to get a better look this time.

I don't think the flower lady can see it.

I get up my courage to talk to it.
"Hello, little one, what are you doing here?"

The little one doesn't say anything back.
It just hops down and trots off.

Where is it going?

In there?
I follow it through the hole
in the fence to find…

so many flowers and plants!

The little one slides one door open
and then the other.
Cl-cl-clap!
Cl-cl-clack!

A cup of tea!
For me?

The little one
doesn't talk very much.

The closet?

Maybe it wants to show me something.

Clack!
Huh? It's empty.

I think I should follow it.

It slides the door shut, and everything goes dark.

I think the little one is closing its eyes,
so I close mine too.

As soon as I do, I can hear something.
The wind is whispering.

Cl-clack!

I open my eyes.
The little one is climbing into the attic.

I follow it up and—

Wow!

Oh, what's that?
A mountain?

The little one
climbs up and up.

This mountain is
so soft and warm.

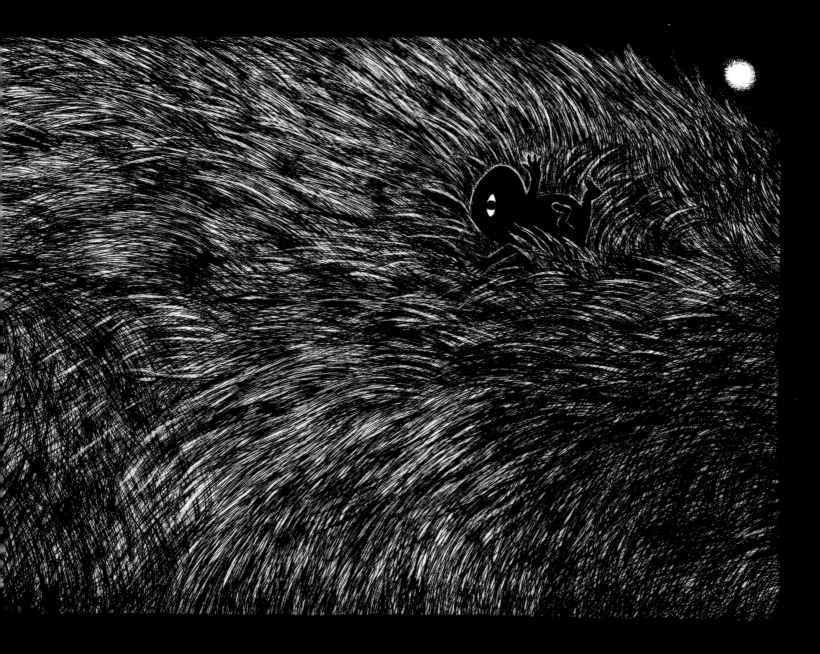

We fall asleep
on the soft warm fur.

I had a dream about my mom.

On the way back,
we walk together,
hand in hand.

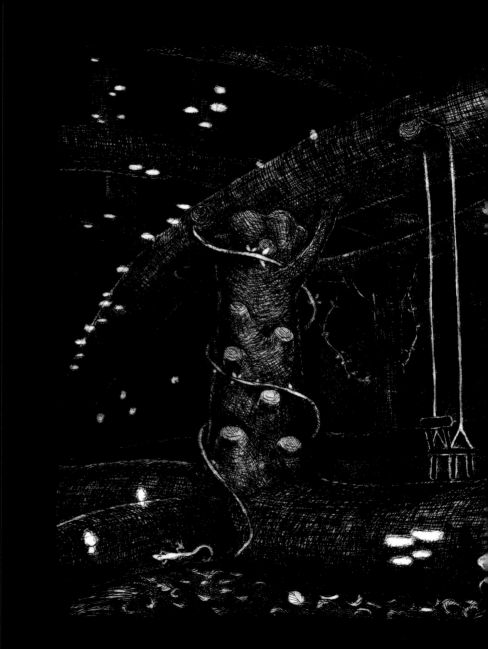

Clack!

Bye-bye, little one!

Mmm, smells good.

Oh! Hi, Daddy!